Clifford
Makes the Team

Norman Bridwell

SCHOLASTIC INC.

It is a sunny day.
Clifford wants to play.

Emerson Library

Clifford
Makes the Team

For Jean Bryant

The author would like to thank Frank Rocco and Grace Maccarone
for their contributions to this book.

Copyright © 2011 by Norman Bridwell.

All rights reserved. Published by Scholastic Inc.
SCHOLASTIC, CARTWHEEL BOOKS, and associated logos
are trademarks and/or registered trademarks of Scholastic Inc.
CLIFFORD, CLIFFORD THE BIG RED DOG, BE BIG, and associated logos are
trademarks and/or registered trademarks of Norman Bridwell.
Lexile is a registered trademark of MetaMetrics, Inc.

No part of this publication may be reproduced, stored in a retrieval system, or transmitted in any form or by any
means, electronic, mechanical, photocopying, recording, or otherwise, without written permission of the publisher.
For information regarding permission, write to Scholastic Inc.,
Attention: Permissions Department, 557 Broadway, New York, NY 10012.

Library of Congress Cataloging-in-Publication Data is available.

ISBN 978-0-545-23141-1

14 13 12 11 10 9 8   14 15 16 17 18 19/0

Printed in the U.S.A. 40
First printing, January 2011

Clifford sees a boy.
He has a bat.

Clifford sees a girl.
She has a bat, too.

Clifford follows
them to the park.

The children play ball.

They have fun.
Clifford wants to play, too.

Clifford looks for a bat.
He sees a tree.

Can he use that as a bat?

No. The tree has branches.

Clifford puts it back.

Clifford sees a pole.
Can he use that as a bat?

No. The pole has wires.

Clifford puts it back.

Clifford sees a pipe.
Can he use that as a bat?

No. The workers do not want
Clifford to take the pipe.

Clifford puts it back.

Clifford goes back
to watch the game.

He is sad. He is crying.
The boys and girls are
getting wet.

A boy says,
"I think Clifford wants to play."

The boys and girls want
Clifford to play.
They make up a new game.
They call it Clifford baseball.

The boys and girls hit and pitch.
Clifford plays first base, second base,
third base, and shortstop.

Clifford plays left field,
center field, and right field.

Everyone wins with Clifford!